SOUTH DAKOTA

EXPLORE THE UNITED STATES

Sarah Tieck

Big Buddy BOOKS

Explore the United States

VISIT US AT
www.abdopublishing.com

Published by ABDO Publishing Company, PO Box 398166, Minneapolis, MN 55439.

Printed in the United States of America, North Mankato, Minnesota.
052012
092012

PRINTED ON RECYCLED PAPER

Coordinating Series Editor: Rochelle Baltzer
Contributing Editors: Megan M. Gunderson, Marcia Zappa
Graphic Design: Adam Craven
Cover Photograph: *Shutterstock*: Olivier Le Queinec.
Interior Photographs/Illustrations: *Alamy*: North Wind Picture Archives (p. 13), Don Smetzer (p. 23); *AP Photo*: AP Photo (p. 13), Richard Drew (p. 25); *CORBIS*: ©Bettmann (p. 23); *Glow Images*: Superstock (p. 9); *Horticulture Photography*: ©Muriel Orans/Horticulture Photography™ (p. 30); *iStockphoto*: ©iStockphoto.com/jameslee999 (p. 19), ©iStockphoto.com/karenparker2000 (p. 27), ©iStockphoto.com/oversnap (p. 27), ©iStockphoto.com/Terryfic3D (p. 26); *Shutterstock*: Anton Foltin (p. 5), Lijuan Guo (p. 30), Barnes Ian (p. 17), Philip Lange (p. 30), Evan Meyer (p. 29), Caitlin Mirra (pp. 26, 27), Jim Parkin (p. 21), Tom Reichner (p. 30), Harris Shiffman (p. 11), solpo (p. 9), trekandshoot (p. 21).

All population figures taken from the 2010 US census.

Library of Congress Cataloging-in-Publication Data

Tieck, Sarah, 1976-
  South Dakota / Sarah Tieck.
    p. cm. -- (Explore the United States)
  ISBN 978-1-61783-380-9
  1. South Dakota--Juvenile literature. I. Title.
  F651.3.T54 2013
  978.3--dc23
                        2012017003

Contents

ONE NATION

The United States is a **diverse** country. It has farmland, cities, coasts, and mountains. Its people come from many different backgrounds. And, its history covers more than 200 years.

Today the country includes 50 states. South Dakota is one of these states. Let's learn more about this state and its story!

Did You Know?

South Dakota became a state on November 2, 1889. It was the fortieth state to join the nation.

Custer State Park is one of the state's natural wonders. It is home to many bison.

SOUTH DAKOTA UP CLOSE

The United States has four main **regions**. South Dakota is in the Midwest.

South Dakota shares its borders with six other states. North Dakota is north. Minnesota and Iowa are east. Nebraska is south. Wyoming and Montana are west.

South Dakota has a total area of 77,116 square miles (199,730 sq km). About 814,000 people live there.

Did You Know?

Washington DC is the US capital city. Puerto Rico is a US commonwealth. This means it is governed by its own people.

REGIONS OF THE UNITED STATES

Legend:
- = West
- = Midwest
- = South
- = Northeast

CANADA

WASHINGTON
MONTANA
NORTH DAKOTA
MINNESOTA
VERMONT
MAINE
NEW HAMPSHIRE
OREGON
IDAHO
WYOMING
SOUTH DAKOTA
WISCONSIN
MICHIGAN
NEW YORK
MASSACHUSETTS
RHODE ISLAND
CONNECTICUT
PENNSYLVANIA
NEW JERSEY
IOWA
OHIO
NEBRASKA
ILLINOIS
INDIANA
Washington DC ★
DELAWARE
MARYLAND
WEST VIRGINIA
VIRGINIA
NEVADA
UTAH
COLORADO
KANSAS
MISSOURI
KENTUCKY
PACIFIC OCEAN
CALIFORNIA
NORTH CAROLINA
TENNESSEE
ATLANTIC OCEAN
ARIZONA
NEW MEXICO
OKLAHOMA
ARKANSAS
SOUTH CAROLINA
MISSISSIPPI
GEORGIA
TEXAS
LOUISIANA
ALABAMA
FLORIDA
GULF OF MEXICO

ALASKA

MEXICO

HAWAII

PUERTO RICO

N
W   E
S

7

Important Cities

Pierre (PIHR) is South Dakota's **capital**. It is located along the Missouri River. Historic **Fort** Pierre is nearby.

Sioux (SOO) Falls is the largest city in the state. It is home to 153,888 people. This city is on the Big Sioux River. It was named for the river's large waterfall.

South Dakota's capitol was completed in 1910.

Pinkish-brown rock surrounds the falls of the Big Sioux River. This type of rock was used for buildings in the area.

South Dakota

Aberdeen●

★Pierre

●Rapid City

Sioux Falls●

N
W   E
S

Rapid City is South Dakota's second-largest city. It has 67,956 people. The city is near the Black Hills and Mount Rushmore. Many people vacation there.

Aberdeen is the state's third-largest city, with 26,091 people. It has a historic Main Street. The city is home to Wylie Park, where people can bike, picnic, and mini golf.

Rapid City is considered the gateway to the Black Hills.

South Dakota in History

South Dakota's history includes Native Americans and explorers. Native Americans lived on the land for thousands of years before others arrived. Many hunted bison. Others grew crops.

In 1682, French explorers claimed what is now South Dakota. In 1803, the United States bought much of this land as part of the **Louisiana Purchase**. After years as a US territory, South Dakota became a state in 1889.

President Thomas Jefferson arranged for the Louisiana Purchase.

In 1874, gold was discovered in the Black Hills. As more gold was found, mining towns such as Deadwood were created.

THE BIG HORN STORE

TAILOR SHOP

Timeline

1803

President Thomas Jefferson arranged for the United States to buy land in the **Louisiana Purchase**. It included most of present-day South Dakota.

1861

Congress created the Dakota Territory.

1890

After years of fighting over land, US soldiers killed hundreds of Native Americans near Wounded Knee Creek.

1800s

Meriwether Lewis and William Clark began to explore what is now South Dakota.

1804

The Dakota Territory became two states on November 2. North Dakota was the thirty-ninth state. South Dakota was the fortieth state.

1889

14

1966

Four dams on the Missouri River were completed to provide power to South Dakota.

2011

Heavy snowfall caused historic spring flooding in South Dakota. This destroyed homes and roads.

1900s

2000s

Work started on Mount Rushmore.

1927

Native Americans held a **protest** for 71 days at Wounded Knee. They did this to get better treatment from the US government.

1973

ACROSS THE LAND

South Dakota has thick forests, low mountains, grassy **plains**, caves, rivers, and lakes. Major rivers include the Missouri and the Big Sioux. The Black Hills and the Badlands are in western South Dakota.

Many types of animals make their homes in this state. These include white-tailed deer, pronghorns, bass, and ring-necked pheasants.

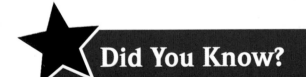

Did You Know?

In July, the average temperature in South Dakota is 74°F (23°C). In January, it is 16°F (-9°C).

The Badlands are known for unusual rock formations. They have been shaped by water over many years.

EARNING A LIVING

South Dakota has many important businesses. People work in banks, schools, and hospitals. The state is one of the country's most popular vacation spots. So, a lot of people have jobs helping visitors.

South Dakota has many natural **resources**. Its mines provide cement, sand, and stone. Farms cover much of the land. Wheat, soybeans, and corn are major crops.

Many South Dakota farms produce hay (*above*), oats, or livestock.

Natural Wonder

The Black Hills National Forest is in southwestern South Dakota and part of Wyoming. This is a popular vacation spot. It is famous for its rock cliffs, pine forests, and grassy **plains**.

For many years, Native Americans lived in this area. After gold was found in 1874, settlers arrived. In 1897, President Grover Cleveland set aside this land. It became the Black Hills National Forest in 1907. Today, people camp, hike, and ride motorcycles there.

Did You Know?

The Black Hills look dark from a distance. That is how they got their name.

Harney Peak is in the Black Hills. It is the state's highest point, at 7,242 feet (2,207 m).

Visitors can climb Harney Peak for a great view of Black Hills National Forest.

Hometown Heroes

Many famous people have lived in South Dakota. Laura Ingalls Wilder was born in Pepin, Wisconsin, in 1867. Her family claimed a **homestead** in De Smet in 1880.

Wilder wrote novels about her family's life. She became known for books such as *Little House on the Prairie*. Wilder wrote *By the Shores of Silver Lake, The Long Winter*, and *Little Town on the Prairie* about South Dakota.

Did You Know?

Wilder married her husband, Almanzo Wilder, in De Smet in 1885.

Each year, about 20,000 people visit the Ingalls Homestead in De Smet.

Wilder's first book came out in 1932.

23

Tom Brokaw was born in Webster in 1940. He is a famous television reporter. He led *NBC Nightly News* from 1982 to 2004.

Brokaw is also an author of several books. In 2002, he wrote *A Long Way from Home*. It is about growing up in South Dakota.

Did You Know?

Brokaw attended the University of South Dakota in Vermillion. He worked in radio stations in the area.

Brokaw became known for reporting news in a calm, clear way.

Tour Book

Do you want to go to South Dakota? If you visit the state, here are some places to go and things to do!

 **See**

Walk around the Corn Palace in Mitchell. This famous building features art made of corn, grains, and grasses. The first Corn Palace was built in 1892.

★ **Play**

Spend time in the Black Hills. Look for wild animals, such as bison. And, stop for trail hikes. You can even swim in the cool waters of Sylvan Lake (*right*)!

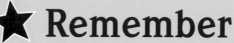
★ Remember

Visit the old mining town of Deadwood. There, you can see what life was like during South Dakota's gold rush.

★ Discover

Explore underground at Jewel Cave or Wind Cave. Both are among the world's longest cave systems!

★ Explore

See herds of wild horses in the Black Hills Wild Horse Sanctuary. The grounds also have old frontier homes and Native American drawings called petroglyphs (PEH-truh-glihfs).

A GREAT STATE

The story of South Dakota is important to the United States. The people and places that make up this state offer something special to the country. Together with all the states, South Dakota helps make the United States great.

South Dakota is known for Mount Rushmore. The faces of four presidents are carved into this famous cliff. They are George Washington, Thomas Jefferson, Theodore Roosevelt, and Abraham Lincoln.

Fast Facts

Date of Statehood:
November 2, 1889

Population (rank):
814,180
(46th most-populated state)

Total Area (rank):
77,116 square miles
(17th largest state)

Motto:
"Under God the People Rule"

Nickname:
Mount Rushmore State

State Capital:
Pierre

Flag:

Flower: American Pasqueflower

Postal Abbreviation:
SD

Tree: Black Hills Spruce

Bird: Ring-Necked Pheasant

Important Words

capital a city where government leaders meet.

diverse made up of things that are different from each other.

fort a building with strong walls to guard against enemies.

homestead a piece of land given to settlers by the US government.

Louisiana Purchase land the United States purchased from France in 1803. It extended from the Mississippi River to the Rocky Mountains and from Canada through the Gulf of Mexico.

plains flat or rolling land without trees.

protest an event where people speak out against or object to something.

region a large part of a country that is different from other parts.

resource a supply of something useful or valued.

Web Sites

To learn more about South Dakota, visit ABDO Publishing Company online. Web sites about South Dakota are featured on our Book Links page. These links are routinely monitored and updated to provide the most current information available.

www.abdopublishing.com

Index